CLEVER CROW

Wäk Liya-Djambatj

In the spirit of respect, I acknowledge Yolŋu elders past and present, the custodians of the land and seas of North East Arnhem Land, for protecting and preserving Yolŋu languages, and for enabling us to learn from and enjoy these languages today.

NL

To my beautiful daughter Ella who is clever,
is always flying and is black.
And to all the children in the world,
may there be love in your life.

BB

CLEVER CROW

Wäk Liya-Djambatj

Nina Lawrence

Illustrated by

Bronwyn Bancroft

Magabala Books

The language of this story

Clever Crow is presented in English and Djambarrpuyŋu.

Djambarrpuyŋu is one of the many Yolŋu languages of the Indigenous people of North East Arnhem Land. More specifically, it belongs to the people of the Dhuwa moiety. The use of Djambarrpuyŋu in *Clever Crow* has been guided and supported by Yolŋu Elders.

It is a pleasure to share this story and to acknowledge and respect a language that has continuously existed in North East Arnhem Land for more than 40,000 years.

Once there was a very hungry crow.

Ŋäthil nhinan gan wäk l̲iya-djambatj. Ŋayi djan̲ŋarrthin mirithin bala

ŋayi marrtjin ŋathalil.

Ŋayi l̲arruŋal ŋathaw dharpaŋur ga mulmuŋur. Bäyŋu!

He searched in the trees and in the grass, but he couldn't find any food.

Then he saw some people at a ceremony. The young men were dancing, and their mother was making a fire to cook a turtle egg.

Bala wäkthu nhäŋal yolŋu'yulŋuy buŋgulŋur. Buŋgulŋur yawirriny' gan giritjin.

Ŋändiy gan baltjam'thurr. Ŋayi djälthin ŋayi dhu bathan mapu miyapunu.

The crow looked at the big turtle egg and cried, 'Yummy, food for me!'

Ŋayi ŋunhi wäkthu nhäŋal ŋunhi mapu miyapunu yindiŋur bathiŋur. Wäk bitjarr waŋan, Garrukalyu dharpaŋur gitkitthurr mirithin.

He stole the egg from the basket and flew into a tree, where a kookaburra was resting.

'Latju ŋatha ŋarraku!' Wäkthu manaŋin ŋunhi mapu bala ŋayi ganydjarryu ŋäl̲'yurr dharpalil.

The kookaburra laughed when he saw the turtle egg.

'Hey, hey, hey!' squawked the crow in surprise, and the egg fell out of his beak ...

Balanyamirriy garrukal gitkitthurr, wäk barrarin mirithin bala bitjarr yatjurr,

'Wäy! Wäy! Wäy!' Bala mapu miyapunu galkirrin wäkkal ŋurruŋur.

… into the pouch of a wallaby
standing under the tree.

Weṯi gan dharran dhuḏiŋur dharpaŋur. Mapu miyapunu gärrin bathilil weṯiwal.

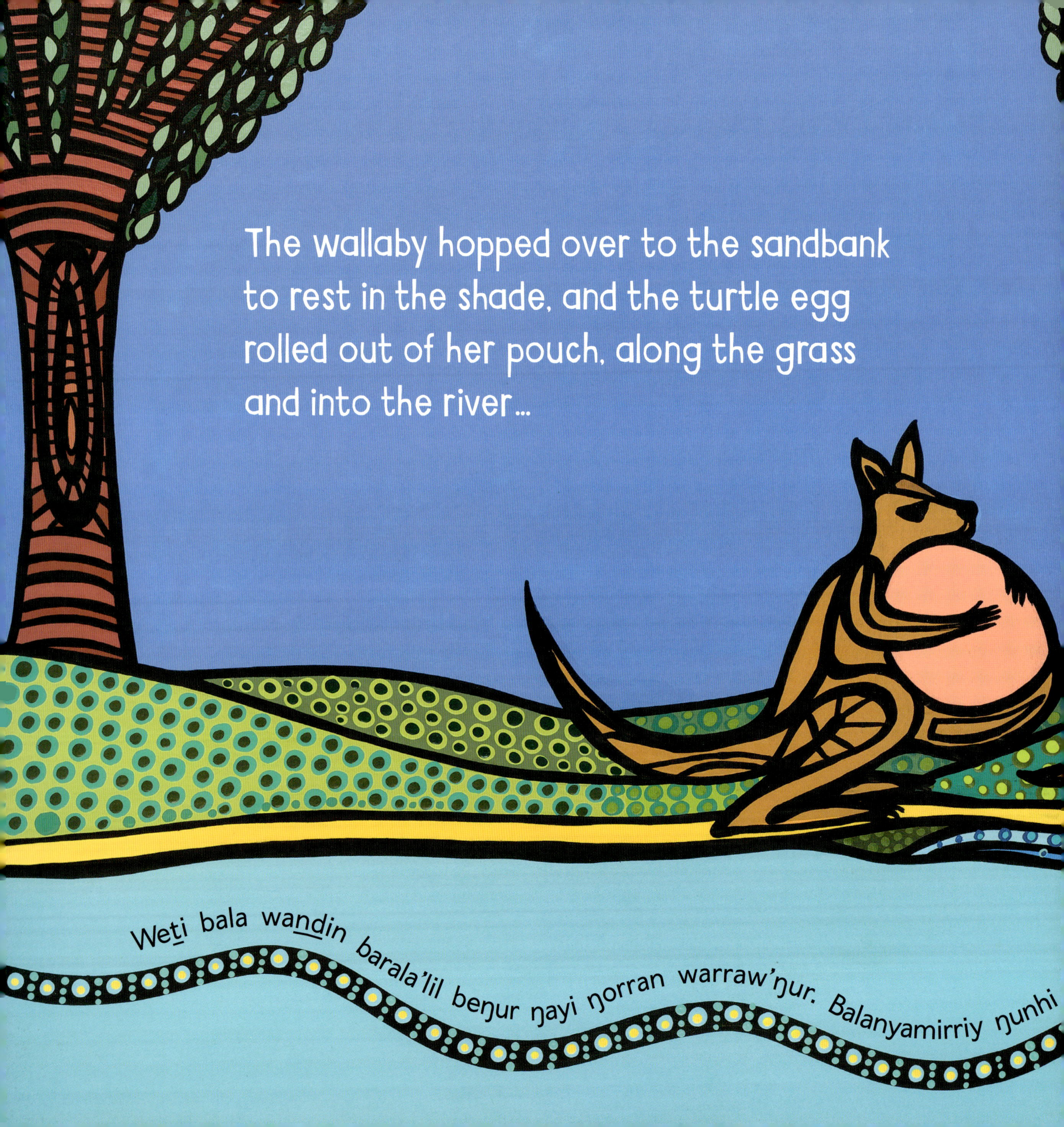

The wallaby hopped over to the sandbank to rest in the shade, and the turtle egg rolled out of her pouch, along the grass and into the river...

Weṯi bala waṉḏin barala'lil beŋur ŋayi ŋorran warraw'ŋur. Balanyamirriy ŋunhi

weṯi gan ŋorran, mapu miyapunu galkirrin mulmukurr bala yarrwupthurr gapulil.

Worruŋu gan ḻiw'yurr lipalipay ḻarrunharaw guyaw. Ŋayi nhäŋal mapu gapuŋur bala

...towards an old man who was fishing.
He lifted it into his canoe.

ŋayi l̲aw'maraŋal mapu lipalipalil.

'It's a big turtle egg!' he cried.
'I'll give this to somebody.'

The old man paddled over to the people at the ceremony.

Ŋayi bitjarr waŋan, 'Yindi dhuwal mapu miyapunu. Ŋarra dhu gurrupan dhuwal mapu

ŋula yolnha.' Bala worruŋu marrtjin barala'lil. Worruŋuy nhäŋal yolŋu'yulŋuy buŋgulŋur.

'I found this big egg,' said the old man, and he gave it to the mother. She was happy to have her turtle egg back – but she didn't see the clever crow watching them from the tree.

Ŋayi bitjarr waŋan, 'Dhuwal mapu yindi ŋarra nhäŋal' bala
Ŋäṉḏi djulŋithin mirithin yurr ŋayi wäwu gan nhinan ga wäk ḻiya-djambatj dharpaŋur

ŋayi gurrupar mapu ŋändiwal.
gan ŋanya nhäŋal.

Bala wäkthu mananjin mapu ŋurruy.

Suddenly, the crow flew down and grabbed the egg with his beak.

That clever crow!

He flew far away with the big turtle egg.

Ŋayi wäk l̲iya-djambatj! Ŋayi ganydjarryu bala but̲thur barrkulil.

Clever Crow

Once there was a very hungry crow. He searched in the trees and in the grass, but he couldn't find any food.

Then he saw some people at a ceremony. The young men were dancing, and their mother was making a fire to cook a turtle egg.

The crow looked at the big turtle egg and cried, 'Yummy food for me!' He stole the egg and flew into a tree, where a kookaburra was resting.

The kookaburra laughed when he saw the turtle egg. 'Hey, hey, hey!' squawked the crow in surprise, and the egg fell out of his beak into the pouch of a wallaby standing under the tree.

The wallaby hopped over to the sandbank to rest in the shade, and the turtle egg rolled out of her pouch, along the grass and into the river towards an old man who was fishing. He lifted it into his canoe.

'It's a big turtle egg!' he cried. 'I'll give this to somebody.' The old man paddled over to the people at the ceremony.

'I found this big egg.' said the old man, and he gave it to the mother. She was happy to have her turtle egg back — but she didn't see the clever crow watching them from the tree.

Suddenly the crow flew down and grabbed the egg with his beak. That clever crow! He flew far away with the big turtle egg.

Wäk L̲iya-Djambatj

Ŋäthil nhinan gan wäk l̲iya-djambatj. Ŋayi djan̲ŋarrthin mirithin bala ŋayi marrtjin ŋathalil. Ŋayi l̲arruŋal ŋathaw dharpaŋur ga mulmuŋur. Bäyŋu.

Bala wäkthu nhäŋal yolŋu’yulŋuny buŋgulŋur. Buŋgulŋur yawirriny’ gan giritjin. Ŋän̲d̲iy gan baltjam’thurr. Ŋayi djälthin ŋayi dhu bathan mapu miyapunu.

Ŋayi ŋunhi wäkthu nhäŋal ŋunhi mapu miyapunu yindiŋur bathiŋur. Wäk bitjarr waŋan, ‘Latju ŋatha ŋarraku!’ Wäkthu manaŋin ŋunhi mapu bala ŋayi ganydjarryu ŋäl̲’yurr dharpalil. Garrukalyu dharpaŋur gitkitthurr mirithin.

Balanyamirriy garrukal gitkitthurr, wäk barrarin mirithin bala bitjarr yatjurr ‘Wäy! Wäy! Wäy!’ Bala mapu miyapunu galkirrin wäkkal ŋurruŋur. Wet̲i gan dharran dhud̲iŋur dharpaŋur. Mapu miyapunu gärrin bathilil wet̲iwal.

Wet̲i bala wan̲d̲in barala’lil beŋur ŋayi ŋorran warraw’ŋur. Balanyamirriy ŋunhi wet̲i gan ŋorran, mapu miyapunu galkirrin mulmukurr bala yarrwupthurr gapulil. Worruŋu gan liw’yurr lipalipay l̲arrunharaw guyaw. Ŋayi nhäŋal mapu gapuŋur bala ŋayi l̲aw’maraŋal mapu lipalipalil.

Ŋayi bitjarr waŋan, ‘Yindi dhuwal mapu miyapunu. Ŋarra dhu gurrupan dhuwal mapu ŋula yolnha.’ Bala worruŋu marrtjin barala’lil. Worruŋuy nhäŋal yolŋu’yulŋuny buŋgulŋur.

Ŋayi bitjarr waŋan, ‘Dhuwal mapu yindi ŋarra nhäŋal’ bala ŋayi gurrupar mapu ŋän̲d̲iwal. Ŋän̲d̲i djulŋithin mirithin yurr ŋayi wäwu gan nhinan ga wäk l̲iya-djambatj dharpaŋur gan ŋanya nhäŋal.

Bala wäkthu manaŋin mapu ŋurruy. Ŋayi wäk liya-djambatj! Ŋayi ganydjarryu bala but̲thurr barrkulil.

Orthography

Djambarrpuyŋu uses an orthography of 31 sounds which includes 6 vowels and 25 consonants. Although some sounds have no English equivalent, examples are given to the closest possible sounds in English for the purpose of simplicity.

Vowels

a	Like the ‘a’ sound in ‘ago’ or ‘acoustic’
i	Like the ‘i’ sound in ‘tin’ or ‘quick’
u	Like the ‘u’ sound in ‘pull’ or the ‘oo’ sound in ‘good’
ä	Like the ‘a’ sound in ‘father’ or ‘charm’
e	Like the ‘e’ sound in ‘pear’ or the ‘i’ sound in ‘air’
o	Like the ‘o’ sound in ‘bought’ or ‘organic”

Consonants

b	Like the ‘b’ sound in ‘bark’
dh	Like the ‘d’ sound in ‘don’t’
d	Like the ‘d’ sound in ‘mad’
d̲	Like the ‘dd’ sound in ‘paddock’
dj	Like the ‘dg’ sound in ‘badge’

g	Like the ‘g’ sound in ‘haggle’
k	Like the ‘k’ sound in ‘packet’
l	Like the ‘l’ sound in ‘halt’
l̲	Like the ‘l’ sound in ‘curl’
m	Like the ‘m’ sound in ‘make’
n	Like the ‘n’ sound in ‘net’
n̲	Like the ‘n’ sound in ‘carnal’
nh	Like the ‘n’ sound in ‘arranged’
ny	Like the ‘in’ sound in ‘coin’
ŋ	Like the ‘ng’ sound in ‘ring’
p	Like the ‘p’ sound in ‘uptown’
rr	Like the rolled ‘r’ sound in Scottish pronunciation of ‘great’
r	Like the rolled ‘r’ sound in American pronunciation of ‘or’
th	Like the ‘tt’ sound in ‘butter’
t	Like the ‘t’ sound in ‘utmost’
t̲	Like the ‘tt’ sound in ‘Rottnest’
tj	Like the ‘tch’ sound in ‘catch’
w	Like the ‘w’ sound in ‘was’
y	Like the ‘y’ sound in ‘yes’
‘	Sound stop like the break between the words in the phrase ‘a egg’

Glossary

bala	then
bala butthurr	flew away
balanyamirriy	at that moment
baltjam'thurr	cooking
barala'	sandbank
barrarin	startled
barrkulil	far away
bathan	cook
bathi	basket, pouch
bathiŋur	in the basket
bäyŋu	nothing
beŋur	then
bitjarr	like this
buŋgul	ceremony
buŋgulŋur	at the ceremony
butthurr	flew
dharpa	tree
dharpaŋur	in/from the tree(s)
dharran	standing
dhu bathan	going to cook
dhu gurrupan	going to give
dhudi	base
dhudiŋur	at the base
dhuwal	this
djäl	want
djälthin	wanted
djannarrthin	hungry
djulŋithin	happy
ga	and
galkirrin	fell
gan	was...
gan baltjam'thurr	was cooking
gan dharran	was standing
gan giritjin	was dancing
gan liw'yurr	was paddling
gan nhäŋal	was watching
ganydjarr	quickly
gapu	water
gapuŋur	in the water
gärrin	entered
garrukal	kookaburra
giritjin	dancing
gitkitthurr	laughed
gurrupar	gave
guya	fish
larruŋal	looked, searched
larrunharaw	looking (for)
latju	yummy
law'maraŋal	lifted
-lil	to, towards, into

lipalipa	canoe
lipalipay	in (a) canoe
liw'yurr	paddling
ḻiya-djambatj	clever
manaŋin	stole
mapu	egg
marrtjin	went
mirithin	very
miyapunu	turtle
mulmu	grass
mulmuŋur	in the grass
ŋäl'yurr	flew
ŋäṉḏi	mother
ŋäṉḏiwal	to the mother
ŋanya	him, her
ŋarra	I
ŋarraku	for me, mine
ŋathalil	to get food
ŋatha	food
ŋäthil	once (upon a time)
ŋayi	he, she
ŋorran	lay down
ŋula yolnha	someone
ŋunhi	that, which
- ŋur	at, in, from
ŋurru	beak
ŋurruŋur	from (the) beak
ŋurruy	with (its) beak
nhäŋal	saw, watched
nhinan	there was
-w	for
wäk	crow
-wal	in, on
waŋan	said, explained
waṉḏin	hopped
warraw'	shade
warraw'ŋur	in the shade
wäwu	unaware
wäy	hey
weti	wallaby
worruŋu	old person
-y	with, the
yarrwupthurr	went down
yatjurr	yelled
yawirriny'	young men
yindi	big
yolŋu'yulŋu	people
yurr	but

Nina Lawrence is a descendant of the Yidinji people of Far North Queensland. She has kinship connections with the Yolŋu people who have given her the Dhuwa skin name, Bilinydjan.

Nina is interested in the preservation and promotion of Indigenous Australian languages, and she is working on an anthology of traditional children's songs in the Yolŋu languages of North East Arnhem Land.

Clever Crow was inspired by her work in the Northern Territory where Aboriginal traditional hunting methods are still used.

Bronwyn Bancroft is a Djanbun clan member of the Bundjalung Nation. She illustrated her first book in 1992 and has worked on 40 children's books.

Bronwyn was the Australian finalist for the Ezra Jack Keats Award for Excellence in Children's Book Illustration (1994), received the Dromkeen Medal for her contribution to Australian literature (2010), and was the Australian finalist for the Hans Christian Andersen Award (Illustrator 2016). She has a Diploma of Visual Arts and masters degrees from the University of Sydney (Studio Practice and Visual Art).

This is a Magabala Book
LEADING PUBLISHER OF ABORIGINAL AND
TORRES STRAIT ISLANDER STORYTELLERS.
CHANGING THE WORLD, ONE STORY AT A TIME.

First published 2018, reprinted 2018, 2020, 2022
Magabala Books Aboriginal Corporation, Broome, Western Australia
W: www.magabala.com E: sales@magabala.com

Magabala Books is supported by the Commonwealth Government through the Australia Council, and the State of Western Australia through the Department of Local Government, Sport and Cultural Industries. Magabala Books would like to acknowledge the support of the Shire of Broome, Western Australia.

Magabala Books is Australia's only independent Aboriginal and Torres Strait Islander publishing house. Magabala Books acknowledges the Traditional Owners of the Country on which we live and work. We recognise the unbroken connection to traditional lands, waters and cultures. Through what we publish, we honour all our Elders, peoples and stories, past, present and future.

Designed by Jo Hunt
Colour reproduction by Splitting Image Colour Studio Pty Ltd
Printed in China by Toppan Leefung Printing Ltd

Cataloguing-in-Publication Data available from the National Library of Australia

A catalogue record for this book is available from the National Library of Australia

Department of Local Government, Sport and Cultural Industries
Government of Western Australia
Lotterywest supported
Australian Government
Australia Council for the Arts
Shire of Broome